CW00871953

CASE FILES

UNS LVED

Strange Tales

Edited By Sarah Waterhouse

First published in Great Britain in 2021 by:

Young Writers
Remus House
Coltsfoot Drive
Peterborough
PE2 9BF
Telephone: 01733 890066
Website: www.youngwriters.co.uk

Printed and bound in the UK by BookPrintingUK
Website: www.bookprintinguk.com
YB0467PZ

FOREWORD

As long as there have been people, there has been crime, and as long as there have been people, there have also been stories. Crime fiction has a long history and remains a consistent best-seller to this day. It was for this reason that we decided to delve into the murky underworld of criminals and their misdeeds for our newest writing competition.

We challenged secondary school students to craft a story in just 100 words on the theme of 'Unsolved'. They were encouraged to consider all elements of crime and mystery stories: the crime itself, the victim, the suspect, the investigators, the judge and jury. The result is a variety of styles and narrations, from the smallest misdemeanors to the most heinous of crimes. Will the victims get justice or will the suspects get away with murder? There's only one way to find out!

Here at Young Writers it's our aim to inspire the next generation and instill in them a love of creative writing, and what better way than to see their work in print? The imagination and flair on show in these stories is proof that we might just be achieving that aim! The characters within these pages may have to prove their innocence, but these authors have already proved their skill at writing!

CONTENTS

Ava Sampson (13)	65
James Briggs (11)	66
Anna Weybourne (12)	67
Milica Jovicic (11)	68
Jacob Hinsliff (12)	69
Timothy Robb (11)	70
Thaaniya Manivannan (13)	71
Luke Ellis (13)	72
James Postles (12)	73
Eliisa Patel (12)	74
Poppy Turner (12)	75
Taylor Williams (12)	76
Annie Robinson (11)	77
Lucy White (12)	78
Oliver Fairless (12)	79
Sameer Mohammed (12)	80
Yasmin Barnes (12)	81
Ayesha Iqbal (12)	82
Tom Lucas (13)	83
Kai Radmore (13)	84
Lucy Mills (12)	85
Raakesh Hariram (12)	86
Nathan Durn (12)	87
Amos Kamp (12)	88
Charlotte Hurn (11)	89
Olivia Dunn (11)	90
Luca Lubbat (13)	91

Marden High School, North Shields

Anna Gurney (11)	92
Stirling Griggs (12)	93
Libby Vella (11)	94
Molly Payne (15)	95
Chloe Sherriff (15)	96
Miley Barber (11)	97
May Cademy-Clementson (11)	98
Ankitha Ramesh (12)	99
Moumi Fabima (11)	100
Heather Marchbank (12)	101
Darcy Ridgway (11)	102
Jack Harker (13)	103
Jack Horsham (11)	104

Tarah Mawson (13)	105
Finn O'Brien (12)	106
Harmony Stavers (11)	107
Marnie Boden (11)	108
Neve Campbell (12)	109
Daniel Ward (11)	110
Emma Mills (11)	111

Perryfields High School, Oldbury

Evangeline Perry (11)	112
Lottie Brooks (13)	113
Tilly Wise (13)	114
Vusimuzi Ncachiwe (13)	115
Ethan Brooks (12)	116
Cara Jones (14)	117
Taher Etel (12)	118
Evie Thomas (12)	119
Tegan Jeanes (13)	120
Grace Bell (12)	121
Lucas Willacy (12)	122
Afnaan Asnain (12)	123
Kyle Marklew-Hill (12)	124
Esme Day (13)	125
Rio Moyo (11)	126
Peter Starkie	127
Hayden Weston (11)	128
Emela Branston (12)	129
Lauren Cross (11)	130
David Akinbode (11)	131
Chloe Whitehead (13)	132
Jensen Warren (11)	133
Leveah Anning	134
Sadie Jean (12)	135
Alfie Redfern-Webb (12)	136
Georgia Byfield-Cable (13)	137
Lauren Moores (12)	138
Grace Brown (13)	139
Simran Kaur Sandhu (11)	140
Ellie Shier (12)	141
Ethan Elliott (11)	142
Josh Messer (12)	143
Kai'sean Mattis (12)	144
Megan Sanders (11)	145

Evie Morris (13)	146	Annalise Baldock (12)	186
Oliver Kapasi (13)	147		
Dexter Gooding (11)	148		
Alexander Jongwe (12)	149		

Rugby Free Secondary School, Rugby

Courtney Rigby (14)	150
Wiktoria Groszewska (13)	151
Madison Bramwell (11)	152
Nadia Barnor (12)	153
Hannah Parrish (12)	154
Jason Zhang (15)	155
Ashton Castleton (12)	156
Patricija Biseniece (13)	157
Jonathan Middleton (15)	158
Cailey Adams (14)	159
Leah Chamberlain (13)	160
Charlee O'Meara (15)	161
Lucy Carlyon (12)	162
Lilly Barker (13)	163
Niamh Evans (13)	164
Emanuele Paval (13)	165
Eliona Seraj (16)	166
Arani Niranjan (12)	167
Keeley Prestidge (12)	168
Coby Smith (11)	169
Bethan Pybus (14)	170
Shakira Rogrigues-Fahrina (14)	171
Amelia Richardson (14)	172
Imogen Page (13)	173
Steffi Moser (13)	174
Thomas Jebson (15)	175
Anastasia Gkika (12)	176
Bethany Bradshaw (13)	177
Holly Prestidge (13)	178
Zainab Malik (13)	179
Dominik Tarnowski (13)	180
Rafi Khan (12)	181
Brooke Herrington (12)	182
Jackie Williams (14)	183
Jack Pearson (15)	184
Elise Richardson (15)	185

THE STORIES

UNSOLVED

She's dead. That girl. The one who was confident, in all the school plays, actually capable of holding a conversation without weeping stupidly. She was great. She used to smile all the time; had a small bubble of friends, but really, she could have had anyone. Flawless in anything she wore and an A* student. She's really missed.

Nobody knows what happened to her. Who killed her and why she was replaced by tears? An introverted geek, crying all the time, won't open up to anyone. Needs constant support, yet pushes her closest friends away.

Nobody knows why I changed.

Jorja Hughes (13)

Blessed Thomas Holford Catholic College, Altrincham

UNSOLVED

I made the floor gleam. The toxic fumes of bleach filled the air. I looked around cautiously and saw it; the once shining silver blade now covered in a vivid unforgettable crimson. The blade lay on the snow-white carpet. The carpet was being poisoned! I panicked. I ran to the kitchen and hastily scurried through one of the drawers. I found a matchbox. Without thinking, I lit a match and threw it into the living room where I'd left the blade! Instantly, smoke filled my lungs as an inferno destroyed everything, including the house. I ran. I was a fugitive...

Harry Ridgway (13)
Blessed Thomas Holford Catholic College, Altrincham

THE CONFESSION

After Phelps told the detective the tale of how his wife was murdered, he was free to go. Phelps began leaving when Slothe spoke.

"How did it feel?"

He stood bewildered by this comment. "Wha-" Phelps began.

"I said, how did it feel to kill your wife. You said someone broke into your bedroom on the top floor?"

"Yes," replied Phelps, trembling.

"So, Mr Phelps, how did someone break into a window on the top floor?"

Phelps retorted, "If you're implying *I* strangled her, you're mistaken."

Detective Slothe then said triumphantly, "No one said anything about strangulation..."

Jack Kerr (14)
Holmer Green Senior School, Holmer Green

MY UNSOLVED CASE

"So, is this where you found the body?"

"Yes."

It was my first case, I was nervous. The poor man was lying on the floor, no longer living.

"Sir, we found a tracker on the victim's phone, we've just located it. Wait, it's moving. It's left the building!"

My radio turned on. "Sir, we see a man leaving the building!"

"Follow him."

The sounds of sirens suddenly awoke the street. The car sped up the road. The man was standing, staring at his next victims.

"Sir, we see him approaching. Oh no-"

The line went dead... We never found them.

Macey Simmonds (11)
Holmer Green Senior School, Holmer Green

KILLER...

It's not fair. Me, a killer? Here's how it went...

"FBI! Open up!" someone bellowed from outside. My blood ran cold. I was just getting up off my seat when a police officer collided with the door and forced it to splinters. Several officers sprinted in, surrounding me. I screamed! I was dragged into the police car, handcuffed behind my back.

Now, here I sit, shivering in a cold cell.

"Guilty."

All because I had a similar Halloween mask. What sort of evidence is that?

Doesn't matter now though. Life imprisonment; I don't even know why.

"Say goodbye to freedom..."

Matilda Thompson (12)

Holmer Green Senior School, Holmer Green

HITMAN JITTERS

We had been given our next victim's file. 37-year-old Jack Davidson, a known thief. He had stolen a total of 123 bottles of Chanel perfume from 64 different locations. Adding up to a total of £9,717. Peculiar. I didn't think much more of it until we arrived at his most recent positioning. "This can't be it!" my sister exclaimed. "Most of our hits live in solitude." We had arrived at a small cottage. "There he is," she whispered, loading a shotgun and handing me a rifle.
"I can't do it," I stated, lowering my gun. "I can't kill him."

Betsy Barcock (13)
Holmer Green Senior School, Holmer Green

BALLROOM MURDER

I looked down at my hands to find my gloves drenched in blood. I looked around in trepidation, frightened someone may have seen me, but saw no one and heard nothing but the faint waltz in the background. People say the dead can't talk, but I heard his voice loud and clear.

"You didn't think this one through, did you? What are you planning on doing now?"

My mind was racing. The thought that came to mind was to cover it up.

"So, do you regret the accident?"

"It wasn't an accident," I told the detective. "My plan was perfect."

Zoe Walastyan

Holmer Green Senior School, Holmer Green

UNSOLVED

"Guilty!"

Bang! At that moment, I was put behind bars. I wasn't even guilty; how do they even know it wasn't the other suspect, Mc Bobothy? I wasn't even near there last night. Maybe the translation for the fingerprint was messed up in the process. It could have even been someone related to me; I just know it wasn't me. I still remember what they said when they were locking me up:

"What a bad mark after a murder, putting the victims' heads down toilets." Flushing heads down toilets? I think that's ridiculous! It can't have been me!

Luke Charleston (11)

Holmer Green Senior School, Holmer Green

THE DIAMOND

"Guilty!" the judge said as Patrick was taken away. He had been framed. Last night, at a museum in London, where he was a security guard, protecting the most valuable artefact, the diamond, he was sleeping when the alarm went off. He saw a robber smashing the glass around the diamond. Patrick put his hand on the glass to try and stop the robber, but the robber knocked Patrick out and escaped through the window.

The next day... 'Breaking news: Extremely rare diamond stolen - suspect found!' Later that day, the report said Patrick's fingerprints were found on the glass...

Lucas Cameron (13)

Holmer Green Senior School, Holmer Green

AHA, FOUND YOU!

The door slammed.

"Another murder, another one!" screamed Mr Oakland who was the city's detective. Out of nowhere, there was a loud scream. Mr Oakland ran into his car and followed the noise. They ended up at an old run-down children's park. There was a fairly young lady lying on the floor, dead, with blood next to her and a business card of a man named Johnathan Scott. Then a memory came back, Mr Oakland remembered. Johnathan used to go to his college. He worked at the city's big office. "Aha!" whispered Mr Oakland. "Found you this time..."

Louisa Reynolds (12)

Holmer Green Senior School, Holmer Green

WHAT HAD HAPPENED?

Troubling times have come... There had been reports of killings on the news every day with the trademark: a cut deep into their heart, with a blood-covered silver dagger. No fingerprints found, just the dagger. There seemed to be a new one every day. The question was, who could have that many daggers?

One day, a discovery was made that could change history forever. A blue plastic glove. Only one, but still vital. The police completed investigations, but still no fingerprints. Who could this horrible person be? Tearing apart families? Tears shed. Funerals were held, mourning the dead.

Daisy Warfield (12)
Holmer Green Senior School, Holmer Green

THE SILENT DEATH

I looked at my mother's cold dead body; another person wrenched out of my hands. Harriet, the head maid, looked at the constable.

"You must know what happened to Lady Weston?"

He sighed and shook his head. Harriet opened her mouth, but no words came out. My cold dead eyes looked around the minimalist room as I slowly took a step forward and walked towards the drawer. It had an unfinished red velvet cake on top of it. I let out a small empty laugh and looked at the constable. "My mother wouldn't just randomly die, she must've been poisoned..."

Haiqa Fatima (13)
Holmer Green Senior School, Holmer Green

THE ASSASSINATION

"Hello? Matt Hancock speaking. Yes, that would be perfect. 1 o'clock okay? Great. See you then."
I was on my way. Our plan was perfect. We had arrived, it was 12:58 and the gates slowly swung open. Our tinted Range Rover slowly drove along the driveway, towards the family mansion. There he was, Matt Hancock. There were no bodyguards or police officers. This would be an easy hit. "Darn it!"
The news was live at the scene. The silencer was found. I must flee the country. It's not safe here, everyone is after me, there is nowhere left to hide...

Finn Clegg (13)
Holmer Green Senior School, Holmer Green

CHEAT THE PAST

The lie detector results were back. It wasn't him, but how? He was there when the crime was committed. The descriptions based on where he was fitted. Could he have hacked the system? No; impossible. It's the most secure program. Maybe I should give up; it's been twenty years. If we haven't solved it yet, we aren't going to. There wasn't anyone else at Titan's Spaceport. Maybe it was a hacker; they could've hacked the shuttle and caused it to crash. Hold on. I think I've got a lead, the hooded figure at the port. It was him, let's go...

Sol Anderson (13)
Holmer Green Senior School, Holmer Green

ON THE RUN

We were in the car. How did they find us? I never thought they'd find us this time, but here we are. I still can't believe they think it's me. Why would I have killed Jessica? I know we got into an argument, but she was still my friend.
"Hey, Scarlett, you in there?" Maddison was talking again.
"Yeah, I'm here, did you need something?"
"No, I just wanted to say that they lost us. Another car looked just like ours and went down another road. They followed that."
We were free again, but for how long?

Meg Waker (12)
Holmer Green Senior School, Holmer Green

THE FIRST DEATH ROW

It started when a disgraceful man was filled with so much jealousy, he decided to kill his wife and children. People saw on the news and thought, *what could've given him the audacity to do such a thing?* The news heading was 'Death Row'. This was something the local people had no clue about and this filled their minds with curiosity. The article said this death row execution would take place on 13/03/1976. Rumours spread that he wasn't the one who killed his family. His lawyers said the same, but who can we believe? Did he kill? We'll never know.

Jacob Gibbs (12)
Holmer Green Senior School, Holmer Green

THE UNSOLVED CASE OF EDITH

Once, back in 1825, there was a lady called Edith. From a very young age, she was obsessed with blood and corpses. Her parents described her as strange and silent. Edith never spoke to anyone until she was twenty-six, and it was about bloody handprints.

In the summer of 1825, Edith was filed as missing by her parents. They found evidence of her being at a shack in the dark woods. After police investigated, they found a man's body.

The police kept tracking her and, at every location she'd been, there was a message on the wall with bloody handprints...

Hannah Sullivan (11)

Holmer Green Senior School, Holmer Green

FRIDAY, 22, 11

Friday, November 22nd, 1963. It was all planned out. Kennedy was going to roll through the plaza and all Jeffory Comradee had to do now was pull the trigger. Two minutes later and it was done. Jeffory's mind was a dark place. He had no remorse.

Three days later, the DPD searched every room and found one thing: a single 50cal metal jacket bullet. The autopsy had revealed the angle at which the bullet entered Kennedy's skull, and like that, the police knew exactly where to look. Raids on his home only found a note saying: 'Tag! You're it now.'

Freddie Eldridge (13)
Holmer Green Senior School, Holmer Green

KIDNAPPED

On one cold evening, a family of six decided to go to the woods. The kids and parents had all their warm, fuzzy clothes on. Several hours later, they came back home and went to bed.

A few weeks later, they were enjoying their hot chocolate when, suddenly, a strange shadowy figure was outside their house. While the parents quickly called the police, the kids decided to head outside and ask the strange man what he was doing. Suddenly, they disappeared. The parents were scared and looked outside. Suddenly, someone put a cloth over them which made them pass out...

Hajra Rashid (11)
Holmer Green Senior School, Holmer Green

"GUILTY OR NOT?"

Some people think the dead can't talk, think or remain, but I'm proof that they can.

As I turned around the corner, I realised it. The truth hit me like a wall made of frozen tears. Could I stay truthful? My name is Johann Finn Hartmann Löwe and I am the top detective in all of Bosnia. When the words 'Are you in?' came from his mouth, I thought that my life was about to get better. Obviously not. Starting the world's oldest mystery was a mistake.

My dad did it! Rokuro Finn Hartmann Löwe.

"Guilty or not?"

Arthur Thomas (14)

Holmer Green Senior School, Holmer Green

THE ASSASSINATION

"Over the wall and into the compound," whispered the leader. In the shadow of darkness, the ninjas almost floated over the wall. Someone slipped a little and their climbing claws scraped, but luckily, no guards came. They were in, they headed straight for the keep of the castle, crossing roofs so not to be spotted by the people. They entered a window high up on the keep and climbed the stairs, straight for the top level. They left no trace of struggle from the lord, so they would think it was poisoning. Like shadows of the night, they floated away...

Harry Holden
Holmer Green Senior School, Holmer Green

UNSOLVABLE

It just didn't add up. Every inch of the scene had been investigated, every centimetre of evidence had been tested and examined, yet there was still nothing. One final, hopeful lead turned into nothing. Although there was one thing that was never checked: a vent. No one noticed a small vent around the corner of the room. As you walked into the room, you would never notice it. The wall to the right covered it up well. "I'm so frustrated! Two months of hard work and nothing came of it."
The murderer heard this. He had never left the scene...

Matthew Timberlake (13)
Holmer Green Senior School, Holmer Green

OPERATION BATEAU

On December the 3rd, a stress call came in from a cargo ship carrying valuable belongings. The boat was coming from South Africa and was going to Portsmouth, England. The message explained that they were being chased by heavily-armed Somalian pirates. The government realised that if they just let the valuable belongings go, they would be in expensive debt. The prime minister called the leader of the SAS and told them to take a squad on a helicopter, and fly them there at night. They dropped in and took out the pirates one by one and delivered the cargo safely.

Patrick Kyte (12)
Holmer Green Senior School, Holmer Green

UNSOLVED

Once, there was a scream. Everyone in that street sprinted to the top office in the town. Everyone was so shocked. They got up the ten-flight staircase and they saw an innocent young woman lying on the floor. Suspiciously, there was a clueless man standing next to her. He immediately got accused of this crime, but he said he was innocent like the rest. The crowd wasn't convinced that what he said was true, so they looked around and they saw another man with a knife. They were both suspicious, but they couldn't finger point at anyone. What a mystery...

Lexi Blunt (11)

Holmer Green Senior School, Holmer Green

SERPENTINE

Bang! The sound of gunshots filled the air! The gunman was the renowned criminal Jim Turner. To know he is a villain, all you have to do is look into his deep black eyes. He was holding a duffle bag, in it 100 million pounds. London wouldn't sleep tonight; all they would hear is the sound of sirens and helicopters flying above them.

Jim worked for an organisation named Serpentine and he had been commanded to collect this money so they could carry out their fatal mission of nuking the world. Millions would be killed. Death was in the air...

Reuben Ramsay (12)

Holmer Green Senior School, Holmer Green

PARADISE ISLAND, OR IS IT?

A murder happened on a wet, rainy night. Detective West was called to investigate the murder of the security guard, Mark Spencer, whose life was ended on the cliff. Detective West was on the case, speaking to the residents of the island. She went to investigate the crime scene and found... a bloodstained earring, broken glass and broken fences. She was led to believe that Mark had knowledge of the wealthy family he worked for. DNA was taken from the blood on the earring and matched to a Patricia Morgan, who's in prison now, but does the story end there?

Jessica Lewington (12)
Holmer Green Senior School, Holmer Green

LIFE OF CRIME!

People say the dead cant walk. Is that true what they say? Well, we are about to find out. There was once a police officer doing his job, checking the neighbourhood when, suddenly, he heard a bang, then next, he heard sirens and lots of voices. He was *dead!* That person was a murderer. One person was accused. She was a witness. A writer, actually. She was the one who called the ambulance for the police officer. Here are her words:
"I would never dare hurt the police force as I respect them dearly." Who could it be? Mystery unsolved!

Aniya Anwar (11)
Holmer Green Senior School, Holmer Green

THE NOTE

It makes no sense. I know that the person we put in prison was framed, and I know who the criminal is, but there is no evidence! The note we found said: 'You still haven't found me.' There were no fingerprints on it though. I don't understand how we have found no evidence that this person did it. Then I remembered... The doorbell! They pressed it when they dropped off the note. They ran, obviously, but they had no gloves on.
Not long later, we arrested them. I was correct! But something was still wrong as we received another note...

Zoe Croucher (12)
Holmer Green Senior School, Holmer Green

UNKNOWN

No one noticed and my body was never found. I was out hunting for clues. The Tailong family were suspected of murder, but they screamed they were innocent.
This is my story.

I was at work, looking for things to investigate. It was weird, how the Tailong family were all killing. Even their children. I went investigating at the place of murder. But something grabbed me and tied me up. They said they would burn and bury my ashes around the world. I realised they killed everyone who came here. They messaged my retirement to my boss and killed me...

Safoora Hafeez (11)

Holmer Green Senior School, Holmer Green

THE NO-LONGER DEAD

People think the dead can't talk. Well, advances in forensic science meant that Robert was shouting beyond the grave. He could only tell one thing, and that was this: people could hear him. They were just too scared to see what was going on. This whole thing was a secret; they would have no clue what was really happening. Then he realised one other thing. The wrong man had been convicted. Matt Hesre, alias of Jack Haldo, was convicted simply because he had done something wrong before, and was let off on that occasion. But who had actually killed him?

Tom Crichton (13)
Holmer Green Senior School, Holmer Green

UNSOLVED

People used to say that a long time ago, the town of Sunnydale was a very welcoming place. Until something unexpected happened. People started to die. There was no telling what was making them pass away; all everyone knew was that it was spreading fast. As soon as some survivors were evacuated, the town was closed off, never to be visited again. Until now... One detective was told to investigating what was happening, and that was Detective Hampshire. She was called to the abandoned town to see what was going on. Now was the time to leave her old life...

Jessica Taylor (12)
Holmer Green Senior School, Holmer Green

THE BANK OF MYSTERIES

A gunshot fired and echoed around the hall. The smoke continued the burn like the sun. The roof caved in and the money spilled out and exploded out, and scattered around the whole building. The vault was blown open and the entire bank was burned to the floor. All that remained untouched was the one bloody chair.

All that continued to stand were the shadows of ten men and their ghostly auras that fled from this building. However, the auras didn't leave and this became the most haunted place across the entire world. And I was left here to rot.

James Gibson (13)
Holmer Green Senior School, Holmer Green

UNSOLVED

"Guilty!" the judge said. "And that's my final word on it." Off I go, but this doesn't exactly feel right; why am I, instead of Andrew, going to jail? Andrew did everything, not me. He was the one who put me in jail. He betrayed me... I just can't believe my best friend would do that. I mean how would you feel if your best friend did that?

Of course, I obviously escaped; that's how I'm writing in this journal. But sadly, everything is unsolved. I'm pretty sure they're looking for me right now...

Shagana Jenathanathan (12)

Holmer Green Senior School, Holmer Green

UNSOLVED

On a snowy night, a strange thing happened to all the kids in High Wycombe. Nobody knows what happened to the children, but they know that the children got taken away two by two.

The parents were very alarmed. They didn't know where their little bundles of joy had gone. They went outside every night to look for them, but they were nowhere to be seen. Apart from a parent who saw a blue colossal figure standing there with two children in its arms. Then the only thing the parent saw was a blue balloon floating away in the distance...

Lachlann Stevens (12)
Holmer Green Senior School, Holmer Green

THE BOYS

Here I am, in the police station. I didn't even do anything; it was my friends. I told them we shouldn't have gone into that house. But, of course, when *I* say that, I'm apparently too scared to do anything. This can't keep happening, I can't keep getting in trouble with them anymore. They set that house on fire, not me!

Anyway, there's no point in me telling the police that I didn't. Why would they believe me over them? The police are asking me to go and talk to them in a room. I hope this goes well...

Millie Edwards (12)

Holmer Green Senior School, Holmer Green

DEAD

On a stormy day, a ship sailed to land. What was it? Where was it from? Every passenger was dead. Not one survivor. Not even the captain. How did it get here with no person to steer?

The mystery taunted us for centuries. We searched the ship. All we found were bloody dead bodies. They'd been shot! By who, how, where, when? So many questions surrounded my brain. I was in complete shock. What sick person would do this? Taking away the lives of thousands of people, simply for enjoyment? The silence that filled the room was so loud. Who?

Megan Dutton (12)
Holmer Green Senior School, Holmer Green

THE ALLEYWAY OF TERROR

It was a cold night with creatures lurking about in the long dark alleyways of the street. I started to walk down the pitch-black alleyway. I nearly jumped out of my skin as this creature stepped in front of me. I stepped back walking into something. I clutched onto my dagger, looked behind me and what I saw terrified me.

What I had forgotten about were my fingerprints. I dropped the dagger quickly and ran for my life.

Thirty years later, I found myself in a prison cell, but I didn't even kill that thing. What was I doing here?

Jessica Craggs (11)
Holmer Green Senior School, Holmer Green

THE MONSTER OF THE PURRING WOODS

There he hanged, my son. How could this have happened? He was chained to a tree, short, demonic. Surrounding the tree were the mutilated bodies of the cult who sacrificed him. Flesh hanging from the bones, the eyes were still in the sockets. Not nice. Odd thing was, death seemed to be by an animal, same for my son. Claw marks, chunks of flesh missing. What did this to my son? I would have cried, if I didn't hear that purr. I heard it ever since I entered. I finally saw the source: a cat, but taller than me!
"Dinnertime..."

David Read (12)
Holmer Green Senior School, Holmer Green

ONLINE KIDNAPPER

I was on a website where I chatted with a bunch of strangers. I was up late, around 3 in the morning in my semi-detached house. I was mainly skipping a lot of strangers until an error came on a particular stranger. They asked if I was alone. I said no, even though I was. I don't know why I lied, but I did it anyway. They said, 'Interesting'. After I gave vague information to them, creepy music started playing outside! Then they asked if I liked music, 'Lenny?' Lenny was my name. Then someone knocked on my front door...

Isa Iqbal (12)

Holmer Green Senior School, Holmer Green

AMONG US MURDER MYSTERY

It didn't add up. Green was Thrash's top suspect. Thrash looked for clues. There was an ajar vent next to the body. Thrash looked inside the vent and then a knife bolted out and narrowly missed him. He looked at the floor and saw a trail of blood. He followed it until he saw White in storage with blood on his hands and a body next to him. Thrash immediately went to the emergency button and told everyone that he saw White with blood on his hands and Brown's dead body. Everyone voted out White, but White wasn't the imposter.

Kai Bose (11)
Holmer Green Senior School, Holmer Green

CYBERHEIST

It's been fifteen years and they still haven't found out.
My shares are null and void since all my accounts are closed to keep away from the prying eyes that is the US government. The public is loving life with their new phones, cars, mansions and food, and here I am, pondering about what the next move should be. Get a job for new bank accounts? Seems smart, but the government is everywhere; can't go two feet out of your front door without seeing a camera.
And that group sit in jail, cursing me daily for what I did.

Oliver Stephen Gibbs (15)

Holmer Green Senior School, Holmer Green

MYSTERIOUS MYSTERIES!

This is not fair. These days, the laws are unfair and stupid. I'm behind cold dark metal bars, only because I was protecting my family, who were under threat. I would not be let out until the day I die; alone in a wet, smelly prison cell. With rats and cockroaches roaming around, wanting to feast on human flesh. One night, I heard screaming from downstairs and obviously I went down to check up on what was happening. With quick thoughts, I grabbed the sharpest thing and struck it through his back. No one knows what I struck him with!

Harry Jones (12)

Holmer Green Senior School, Holmer Green

THE SOVIET'S CONFESSION

"I swear to tell the truth, the whole truth and nothing but the truth."
It had been twenty-five minutes. I was ordered to reload my rifle and start the engine. As we approached the town, people started to run. The general ordered us not to leave any witnesses. As I jumped out of the Jeep, I let off hundreds of rounds of ammunition, mowing down anyone I laid eyes on. We understood we were committing war crimes and mass genocide. But we had no choice. We hadn't slept or eaten in days. I am not proud of what I did.

Charlie Newens (13)
Holmer Green Senior School, Holmer Green

FBI FAILURE

In America, the FBI's most-wanted bad guy was being hunted down. His name was Luke. Luke Bansie. Luke was the FBI's most-wanted person in America because he had murdered Elizabeth. He was bad. When I say bad, I mean *very* bad, and they wanted to capture him but he didn't want to be captured. The FBI managed to track him down, and he was in jail.

A few weeks later, Luke got away. The FBI couldn't capture him, so he ran and jumped over the fence for the Forbidden Territories. Who knows what is in there...?

Holly Curzon-Tompson (12)
Holmer Green Senior School, Holmer Green

STUMBLING UPON THE BODY

Just as I climbed into bed, I remembered that I left my shawl downstairs in the dining hall. I sighed and left the room. When I was just on the second floor, I found a pool of blood covering the whole bottom three steps, and in the middle of it was the body of Lady Awstings. I shrieked and scampered back upstairs to tell Sophie what I had found. Within five minutes, we were running downstairs to find that I had woken up everyone, except it seems that the caretaker, Jones, and Madam Marsh weren't that tired. They were angry...

Lydia Beaumont (12)

Holmer Green Senior School, Holmer Green

IT'S A MYSTERY

You may think that people don't get away with murder, but this case had the police fooled. A body was found in a warehouse near High Wycombe. The name of the deceased was Pauline Hart, thirty-nine. There was nothing at the scene of the crime except a single note which was found in the deceased's hand, which had a confession on it. The crime was committed by a man going by the name of Jeffery Triangle, but the police have checked the databases for anyone with that name, going back 100 years, and no one goes by that name...

Ella Aves (12)
Holmer Green Senior School, Holmer Green

UNSOLVED

"How long?" I pleaded. I had been here long enough. It was time for her to pay her time.

"Not long now, Cam. I've got a plan." She had lowered her voice.

"What are you going to do?" I responded. She pulled out a plastic wallet with a knife dripping in scarlet-red blood. There it was; the horror of my dreams. The one thing that had put me behind a cell in the first place. But how did she have it? It wasn't her response that woke me from my confusion but the yell of a police officer...

Umaymah Hussain (13)

Holmer Green Senior School, Holmer Green

THE BOUNTY HUNTER

I was at a crime scene that looked to be a murder. The reason I was there is because my target was the one responsible for this murder, so I hoped that I would find some clues about him. On the floor, there were multiple footprints which meant that he had help; most likely bodyguards. As well as the footprints were bullet casings. Now I know he likes guns.

Later that day, I tracked him to his mansion, but something didn't seem right. There was no one there: no bodyguards, no servants and no family. What had happened here?

Kai Reading (15)
Holmer Green Senior School, Holmer Green

THE HEIST

On October the 18th, 2019, a heist was taking place. It was coming to an end when they heard sirens. They got in their car and drove off. When police arrived on the scene, they saw car lights racing into the distance. The cops looked around and saw a winter glove on the floor. They took it and examined it for clues to the culprits of this crime. It led them to a ninety-year-old lady who couldn't have possibly done it, so they let her go. Little did they know, it was actually her and her granddaughter who stole £10,000!

Rose Longmore (12)

Holmer Green Senior School, Holmer Green

THE FINAL JOB

I'd shot him. No remorse, no guilt. I had to head south now to the Sahara Desert and collect my reward. Collins told me to meet exactly at the abandoned oil rig directly in the centre. Once I got on the quickest plane to Egypt, I started to wonder where I would lay low. I remembered I had a friend in Brazil. He was trustworthy. It was already out, the news was written with the title: 'Retired general shot dead by masked man.'

I got my reward, Collins congratulated me. He was impressed. I was finally a free man.

Ali Zaib (12)
Holmer Green Senior School, Holmer Green

THE PRESIDENT

It just didn't add up. The fingerprints, the recordings. Everything led to this one room near where the president makes his speech.

All that lies in this room is a dead man. No sniper, just a dead man. My secretary makes a call and shouts down the phone. I am told to watch the stage and all surrounding buildings. We still haven't been told what is going on. As the president is making his speech, everything seems to go quiet. We hear a loud bang that sends a shiver down my spine. The president drops to the ground...

Sam Arkinson (13)
Holmer Green Senior School, Holmer Green

EXPERIMENT

I ran through the corridor, I could hear them shouting at each other behind me. My hands were hot and sweaty but my head hurt even more. I knew they were clever or they wouldn't have disguised their science experiments as madhouse patients. It was hard to believe that after twelve long years, I would be free, but not entirely. I'll always be on the run; I was their first success. The first one to survive the process. I was out in the cool air, my head still throbbing like a knife had been thrust through it. My name? 1222.

Iona Ingham (12)

Holmer Green Senior School, Holmer Green

THE DETECTIVE WHO KILLED

"Get the door down!" I hear them say. If I don't run, I will get caught. I run. I'm a detective, I was following the case of my late father, but they found my golden chain in his pool where he got shot. Was it me who did it? Yes. Am I going to get caught? No. I'm running down the road. I see light coming from behind me, it's headlights... *Smash!* I feel my body collapse onto the stony ground. The floor is vibrating as heavy footsteps come closer and closer to me. It's the police...

Caitlyn Cadby (12)
Holmer Green Senior School, Holmer Green

UNSOLVED

"Guilty!" they bellowed at me! Just because they found the same fingerprints that I have does not mean they can suggest it was me, being the murderer for the death of Jorden in a run-down cave in the blood-curdling woods. They said that the dead can't talk, but I don't believe that. I feel like Jorden is watching us. The court filled. I saw Ellie peering, she had a smirk on her face. She was also said to be there, in the cave with me at the time, until she disappeared and I never saw her again that night...

Freja Milner (12)

Holmer Green Senior School, Holmer Green

UNSOLVED MURDER CASE

I'd found a clue in the alleyway. "Blood drops." So this can show us where the murder was located. Has the murderer put the body somewhere, or he has taken the body with him so we cannot find it? The thing we have kept looking for is the clue to show where he is located somewhere.

Four days later, a body was reported dead in a car. The person was trying to get away from the murderer. There was a gunshot wound in his head, meaning the murderer had a more dangerous weapon than we'd originally thought...

Lewis Tilbury-Balcrczyk (14)

Holmer Green Senior School, Holmer Green

FALSE INNOCENCE

Innocent! I was appalled, shocked and outraged! I had clear evidence he had killed my best friend and he had slipped out of my hands. Three days after the death of my best friend, my mortal enemy walked up my driveway, but then turned in the opposite way and ran. I had to follow him. He ran through cold,
dark alleyways and up rooftops of buildings. He dropped his phone which I knew would be evidence. I hacked inside of his phone and found photos of the murder. So, I took it to the court.
He got found innocent...

Lexie Vaughan (12)
Holmer Green Senior School, Holmer Green

CAGED DESTINY

I run through the trees with one thought in my mind. *Why did I kill him?* The howls of the police hounds are growing ever nearer, meaning my caged destiny is growing even closer. I turn to see them bounding through the bushes, straight towards me. I stumble and fall. When I next look up, I see the police standing over me.

I was caught. As they cuffed me and walked me to the police car, all I could think is, *why?* Why couldn't I resist the temptation, waited until night? Why did I kill them? Why?

Callum Elsey (13)
Holmer Green Senior School, Holmer Green

THE END

"Time to go." The door of my cell slammed open. I breathed a sigh of relief. This was finally it. My endless days of wallowing in self-pity were over. The metallic taste of blood, the smell of the damp soil and the sound of pleading cries as my victims took their last breath will all be gone. I had endured twenty years of suffering and I couldn't go a day without the memories terrorising me. It was a continuous cycle. But the thing that haunted me the most was that no one will ever forget what I have done.

Amy Dutton (14)

Holmer Green Senior School, Holmer Green

CAUGHT!

A day to live. The organisation gave me a day. They said, "The police will be able to get more information out of you the longer you stay alive." I thought I still had a chance, but no. I will be swallowed into the dark path of death, which most criminals decide to follow. I thought I was so careful during the heist, but I was reckless and sloppy. Nowhere near what I once was. The uncatchable has now been caught. They thought it was impossible. Now my life will be taken by the group that dwells in the shadows...

Isaac Ramdeen (13)

Holmer Green Senior School, Holmer Green

COLD CASE - UNSOLVED MURDER MYSTERY

On the night of March the 29th, 2006, Emma Liner was murdered. To this day, no one knows how she died or who killed her. I brought the case back from the last time we worked on it. We're studying it again. The day she was murdered was a special day, a family tradition. She was sixteen, with a boyfriend of seventeen who disappeared the day she was murdered. She was found on the floor, next to a gun bullet and knife, no gun anywhere. The evidence is confusing. The person who committed the murder is smart and a mystery.

Nyiema-Rose Kidby (11)
Holmer Green Senior School, Holmer Green

GUNSHOT

It was my fault Shane was dead. Maybe if I hadn't gone with my friends, I could've helped him to round the cattle up and he wouldn't be dead. I feel so guilty. I heard about men stealing cattle, but I hadn't heard they killed people. There was a gun found, probably the killer's, but it had been wiped down. How could someone be so ignorant? Earlier, I came home and he wasn't back, so I went to help but I found him in the grass, dead. The cattle had gone as well. Whoever did this was going to pay...

Sonia Aslam (12)

Holmer Green Senior School, Holmer Green

THE UNSOLVED CORNER SHOP BURGLARY

The CCTV gave us a clue, but it wasn't enough. I knew that the person who robbed my shop was definitely worthy of being sent to prison, but I would feel terrible getting the wrong person sent to prison. From the CCTV footage, they had traced it back to just two people. For a split second, I wondered whether I should just accuse one of them at random. In the end, I decided to wait for more evidence to be found. Then I heard a letter go through my letterbox. They had found some fingerprints on the corner shop door...

Oliver Smart (12)
Holmer Green Senior School, Holmer Green

I COULD DIE; WILL IT BE WORTH IT?

The suspect is gone. Something doesn't fit right. If he was the murderer, why would he have had *her* phone on him? No. He can't have been. But where do I start? I need to talk to his brother. He might know how he'd been behaving on the night she died.

That was when I snapped out of my circle of thoughts. A slip of paper had come through the letterbox. 'I will kill you too, Eve.' My legs went to jelly. My heart skipped a beat. I flipped the paper and looked on the other side. Nothing...

Ella Mediratta (13)
Holmer Green Senior School, Holmer Green

NEVER SEEN AGAIN...

It's not fair. I don't know how I got here!

"Jessica?"

"Yes?"

"Where are you?"

"I'm in the basement!"

"Okay, and where is Missy, the person who took us?"

"Ha ha, I'm here, I can hear you. If you carry on, I will stab you!" Missy made us frog soup! "Eat it up then!" They ate it and passed out straight away.

Missy heard the cops coming. She ran straight away... No one ever saw her to this day!

Layla Bushell (12)
Holmer Green Senior School, Holmer Green

THEY GOT WHAT THEY DESERVED

"Thanks for coming in. We will have that guy arrested in no time."
I did it. I walked out the police station with a mighty grin on my face. No one will ever know. He got what he deserved. He betrayed me and didn't do as he was told. So, he paid for it. He shouldn't have messed with me. It's a shame really; he was a good employee to have around. But one little mistake cost him his life. I switched my gun for Edward Smith's knife. I couldn't take the fall. So now they will both pay.

Ava Sampson (13)
Holmer Green Senior School, Holmer Green

THE HEIST

Two years to the day since me and my two friends, Martial and Ewan, had the idea to break into the bank of London and steal millions. We were stood outside the doors, cold air burning my eyes through the mask, stood with my pistol cocked and ready to fill my bag to the top. We kicked down the doors and ran inside, staying ready for people and looking for the vault. After about ten minutes, we had reached the 3ft-thick-steel door. I stood guard while Martial hacked the door open then, a gush of air and we were in...

James Briggs (11)
Holmer Green Senior School, Holmer Green

UNSOLVED

One day, in my small home town that no one really goes to, there was a scream. The scream of murder. The townspeople ran over to the barn where the scream came from. There, lying on the floor, covered in blood, was a young boy. Dead. The young boy was stabbed. That boy was my little brother. As I rushed to the barn after hearing this news, I fell to the floor after seeing him there dead. In shock, I didn't know what to feel. He was gone. Stabbed right in his chest. I felt all different emotions. He's gone.

Anna Weybourne (12)
Holmer Green Senior School, Holmer Green

THE STORY OF THE MISSING GIRL

One Saturday afternoon, there was this girl called Millie, and her mum and dad sent her to the shops to get some food. Millie had this friend who she thought was great, however, she kidnaps people! The girl saw Millie at the shops and started leading her to the forest without Millie even realising. She led Millie to a place where she would never find her way home. Then Millie's parents started to get very worried.

Six hours went by. They called the police and they went searching and could not find her...

Milica Jovicic (11)
Holmer Green Senior School, Holmer Green

ACCUSED

When I was at the scene of the crime, there were three of us there: the victim, the culprit and me. The crime was committed, and I know this sounds silly, but the culprit literally vanished in a poof of smoke. I was the only other person there, so the police naturally gave chase. I hid in a nearby alleyway, but it was no use, the police had dogs tracking me, using the coat I dropped stupidly. They cornered me and shot. I blacked out from blood loss and ended up in here. Prison. How did *you* end up here?

Jacob Hinsliff (12)
Holmer Green Senior School, Holmer Green

UNSOLVED

It was a regular night when I received a phone call from the manager. He sounded extremely faint and scared. I asked him if anything was wrong. He replied, "Whatever you do, never enter that door." After that, the line cut off and there was static.

The next morning, I had a job to do. I grabbed my keys and jumped into my car. Strangely, when I arrived, there were two doors at the front. I recognised the right one and went through, wondering, *is it the door my manager was talking about?*

Timothy Robb (11)
Holmer Green Senior School, Holmer Green

THE RUNAWAY

It happened so quickly, my life changed drastically. I ran. I did not know what to do, so I ran. I did not stop. Thoughts ran through my head like wildfire. *Was I making the right decision? Should I have stayed at home?* I'm innocent. I didn't kill him. Or did I? No, I must not think that. I did not. But one question keeps circling my head: *who would kill Jack?* He is a person who would go out of his own way to help a random stranger. I must find out who killed him and clear my name...

Thaaniya Manivannan (13)
Holmer Green Senior School, Holmer Green

THE DEMON

I am stopped halfway as he steps out of the shadows. I raise my gun, but he says... "This mortal body is becoming weak. I must find something more powerful to possess. I suppose you will do."
"What are you talking about? I'm just a normal human!" I cry back.
"Oh, you know nothing. Good; this makes my plan much easier," he snarls back. He starts to glow and I feel my soul dying inside me as the demon possesses my body. I try to scream, but I just fade away...

Luke Ellis (13)
Holmer Green Senior School, Holmer Green

THE GREAT WRECK

That night, I was sleeping in my cabin aboard the SS Partrige when disaster struck. As the beautiful gold and black cruiser slid through the ocean, I was woken by a disturbing shudder from the hull. Suddenly, red alarms blared and I was rushed out of my bed by a crowd that almost carried me to the deck. Up there, I noticed a giant black shuttle of death coming towards us. I was rushed to a red lifeboat dangling from silver chains, and shoved in by a commander. I felt a jolt as the SS Partrige blew up...

James Postles (12)

Holmer Green Senior School, Holmer Green

YOUR WORST NIGHTMARE

It was a cold day... Everyone was going to school and what seemed like a normal day at school, well, wasn't. As the girl was approaching the door to get in, she slipped on some ice and behind her was her worse nightmare... She turned and saw a man holding a gun with blood dripping down it! She tried to turn and run but was shot in the back by the kidnapper.
She woke up in the hospital, not knowing what was going on, then she heard a window crack and realised who it was. Then she screamed...

Eliisa Patel (12)
Holmer Green Senior School, Holmer Green

UNSOLVED KILLER

There was a chill in the air that cold Saturday morning when he struck. The killer had no name or face; it was like he didn't even exist. The only way to tell it was him was the way he presented the body. A perfect cut in the place of the heart which was removed, and in its place was a note reading: 'The kill count will go up and up.'
Now it is a cold case, but the kill count continues to grow each night. Will anyone ever know who this mystery killer is and when will this end?

Poppy Turner (12)
Holmer Green Senior School, Holmer Green

UNSOLVED

We were all at the house party. When I walked outside, there was a girl sat in the corner. I was filled with curiosity. I slowly walked over to the girl. She turned around, she had blood dripping from her eyes! She noticed me and pounced, I grabbed a knife from the cutlery placed outside and stabbed her in the heart. What had I done? I ran back inside, I looked up and saw the same girl! We locked eyes. I ran out but fell.

I woke up to everyone surrounding me. I saw the same girl smiling...

Taylor Williams (12)
Holmer Green Senior School, Holmer Green

THE MURDERER AND THE VICTIM

I was trembling and scared for my life. Knowing it was getting too much, I did not want to end my life, even though I needed to. Though, I picked up the gun. Shivers ran down my spine and I struggled to breathe. One side of me said, "End it all," as the other said to stay. That did not matter. I had not eaten in days; I could not eat. The door smashed open.

"Police! Police!" It was now or never. Still I am a mystery, as they do not know I am the victim and the murderer.

Annie Robinson (11)

Holmer Green Senior School, Holmer Green

UNSOLVED

It just did not add up. Why would John kill his best friend? It did not make any sense. They had been inseparable since childhood, so what could he have done to get John so mad that he would commit murder? These questions flooded through my head, but I did not know the answers. The only evidence at the scene of the crime was John's fingerprints on the bloodstained curtains. If he did not do it... then I had to find out who did! With no other clues to go on, this was going to be difficult.

Lucy White (12)
Holmer Green Senior School, Holmer Green

DARKNESS

There was once a man who was twenty-six years old. No one liked him because everyone thought he was a psychopath. One day, he was at home and he saw a black figure run across his garden. He thought it could be a deer, a fox or a badger, so he didn't care about it. He then heard scratching on the back door. He was a bit creeped out, so he went to the back door and it was already opened! He started to get scared, so he ran upstairs. Little did he know the black figure was up there...

Oliver Fairless (12)
Holmer Green Senior School, Holmer Green

UNSOLVED

In a gloomy area in London, there was a man called Max. He was twenty-six and a murderer. He worked in a cafe in the day and killed people at night. After a while, his luck ran out and the police were able to get enough evidence to prosecute him. He was found guilty and went to jail for a very long long time, London became a safer city without him.

However, he kept saying, "Why did I get arrested and Jessica didn't?"

Did that mean he wasn't working alone?

Sameer Mohammed (12)

Holmer Green Senior School, Holmer Green

LIES

"Guilty! Guilty I tell you. She is the one who killed my family! She always hated us, it was only a matter of time!" I yelled at the judge.

The judge looked at my neighbour (the person who was thought to have killed my parents and sitter). I smirked as she did, you see, I was the one who killed them. But I put her fingerprints all over the knife I killed them with. As court ended, the neighbour was put in prison. It was said to be a solved crime, but it never was.

Yasmin Barnes (12)

Holmer Green Senior School, Holmer Green

UNSOLVED

Thud... Thud. I listened to my heart beating in my chest. I had been framed. someone had stolen my car and left it at the crime scene. I took a sharp turn around the corner and was faced by a dead end! I looked around and found some wood, a fan and a drill. I quickly gathered them, then found the nearest car. I drove to the beach. I hid in an alley and made my boat. I then pushed the boat out to sea. I swore I would come back and that the person who caused this would pay...

Ayesha Iqbal (12)

Holmer Green Senior School, Holmer Green

KIDNAPPED UNSOLVED CASE

It's been a week... All I remember is being taken from my home when I was playing. They grabbed me and threw me into the van. As we left, all I could see was my playhouse and my teddy lying there silently. They were asking me the names of my parents, I told them. He was on the phone to someone, then he said my name. We stopped, we had arrived in Chicago, 100 miles from home. I peered into a box with a picture of a man and a woman holding a baby, my name written on the back...

Tom Lucas (13)
Holmer Green Senior School, Holmer Green

THE CASINO HEIST

As we landed on the rooftop, we shot the camera and went through the door. We met a guard on the stairs but took him out with a quick bang on the head, with the muzzle of my gun. Lester, now speaking to us on the earpiece, guided us to the vault. After taking out lots of guards and cameras, we were on the vault level. With a quick hack, Lester shut off the lights and we were able to get to the mantrap. Now the run to the vault. The laser drills cut it open and we were in…

Kai Radmore (13)
Holmer Green Senior School, Holmer Green

THE ESCAPE

It was dinnertime and I was making my way back to my cell, and I realised that I had left my plan in the cafeteria. Now was my only chance to get out. I needed it so I could follow the steps. Soon, I remembered I had the guard's key, and this meant I could let myself out of my cell, grab my plan and finally leave this awful place. So, I quietly opened my cell and followed the plan. I got past the guards. I actually can't believe they thought that I was Peter Short...

Lucy Mills (12)
Holmer Green Senior School, Holmer Green

HITMAN

I was walking down this dark alley, casually looking back and forth so that no one spotted me. A lot of questions popped up in my mind. How did I get caught? Why did Lucy frame me? I've never been caught before. The boss is not going to be happy!

Whilst I was dreaming, I didn't realise someone was following me behind. I quickly looked around, pulled my trigger, but wait... Something wasn't right. I looked closer. "Mark? But how...?"

Raakesh Hariram (12)

Holmer Green Senior School, Holmer Green

REGRET

Why did I have to do it all those years ago? I feel so bad about killing my brother with that knife. I was never found out though; no one ever knew who did it, I left no clues. It was just a swift cut across his throat and he fell lifeless to the hard floor. I left the body and when the police found it, I was already gone. No one will ever know I did it. Well, not until I lie down and don't wake up.

I do regret it. It keeps me awake and it haunts me...

Nathan Durn (12)

Holmer Green Senior School, Holmer Green

THE FIGURE

It was 11pm. I was driving home from the airport after arriving back from a holiday. I was just enjoying driving, the radio blaring and the speakers pounding. Suddenly, a masked figure stepped out from a dark alleyway. He was dressed in all black, with a firearm poking out of his coat pocket. He approached the driver in front of me and proceeded to open the door. He dragged the driver out of his Range Rover, shot him twice in the stomach and drove off...

Amos Kamp (12)

Holmer Green Senior School, Holmer Green

UNSOLVED

When I woke up, all that came into my mind was last week. My uncle and I had gone camping in a forest close to our home. Sadly, the fun we were having almost stopped immediately as his face exploded in blood and gore. It was said that it had been a hunter who had accidentally thought he was an animal and shot him. No further research had gone into this crime and, to be honest, I'm glad. I'm glad that no one had seen me do it, of course.

Charlotte Hurn (11)
Holmer Green Senior School, Holmer Green

MURDER MYSTERY...

I shouldn't be here! I should have lied! I could have said he tried to attack me. The closest thing I had found was that knife.

I'm so stupid. Now I'm stuck behind these rusty bars for life! If I had left it longer, I would never have been caught and I know that for a fact! I don't even have a proper bed or toilet! Now look at the state I'm in. I'm going to have to die here...

Olivia Dunn (11)

Holmer Green Senior School, Holmer Green

THE CELL

I went back up to my cell, drowning in my sorrows. How did they catch me? How stupid was I to do that? I just sat there on my bed, frozen. Like everything around me just completely stopped working. I couldn't see anyone. But there was one strange figure across my cell. It just stood there. Just staring at me. It was like it wasn't even human. And it was coming for me...

Luca Lubbat (13)
Holmer Green Senior School, Holmer Green

COURTROOM

I stood in the small box. Great spikes jutted up all around me so I couldn't escape. I didn't want to look up in case I caught the judge's eye.

"Is your full name Haeli Tate?"

"Yes," I answered meekly.

"You have been charged with the murder of sixteen-year-old Harry Slaner, do you plead guilty or not guilty?"

I decided not to answer straight away. I thought through the consequences. I knew which one to choose.

"Guilty," I lied. It was the best option to go with.

"Take her away!" I heard the judge roar. Then it all went black...

Anna Gurney (11)
Marden High School, North Shields

THE PRESIDENT'S LAST NIGHT

News flashed up on my phone: 'The president is dead!' I heard sirens getting louder and closer.

"Get down on the ground!" Realisation hit me. Somehow, they thought I was the impostor among the president's guards. My best friend, Steven, stepped out from the shadows.

"He's not guilty, he was with me all night. I can prove it!"

An officer took Steven's phone from his hand, showing a photograph of us just minutes before. The officer squinted at the photo of the two of us.

"He's telling the truth. I can see the attacker in the background of this photo..."

Stirling Griggs (12)

Marden High School, North Shields

THE INTERVIEW

Lewis sat in the chair, looking at the officers with his dark, deep, menacing black eyes.

"I am Detective Vella and this is Sergeant Winstin. We are here to discuss the murder of Billy Brown. You have been called here today as a suspect." They started the interview. Sergeant Winstin asked in a firm, clear voice, "When was the last time you saw Billy Brown?" Lewis exploded in anger, and banged his fists on the table and screamed, "I don't know anyone called Billy Brown!"

"Lewis, we have evidence on CCTV footage about what happened. You need to explain, Lewis..."

Libby Vella (11)

Marden High School, North Shields

DISCONNECTION FROM JUSTICE

He played the phone call again, listening to every word and sound that was made. It came from a phone found with only the victim's prints on it. All the prints found belonged to the victim. The voice gave the detective chills. It was robotic in nature, like an automated voicemail.

An email popped through from the Forensics lab with the results. It read: 'It's the victim's.'

The handwriting on the note - 'I will not stop!' - found next to the severed hand of the girl was their best hope at catching the culprit.

Their only clue.

Useless.

Molly Payne (15)
Marden High School, North Shields

THE LOST PRINCESS

As I dressed in their clothes, I prepared myself to be thrown into an alternative realm. Surprisingly, I was thrown to the ground, not as gracefully as I imagined. I raised my head to see it. The green and golden castle with all intricate details standing before me. I ran my finger along the details all painted gold, and raised my head further to admire the height of the palace as it was taller than the Eiffel Tower. The grass was green like all the photoshopped pictures you see on the internet. Suddenly, I was greeted, "Welcome home, lost princess!"

Chloe Sherriff (15)
Marden High School, North Shields

UNSOLVED MYSTERIES

Peering through the trees, I saw the blue lights flashing like a beacon and hear sirens blaring, yet there was still an eerie silence in the air.

News had just broken that a child killer was on the run. Babies were wailing, feeling their mothers' tension.

Crowds were beginning to gather, hungry for information. Who is it? Where is he from? Why Cullercoats? A police cordon was being erected. I could hear dogs barking. The dog squad had arrived.

I could feel a warm breath on the back of my neck. I turned around, I was face-to-face with the killer...

Miley Barber (11)

Marden High School, North Shields

A NORMAL CASE OR SO THEY THOUGHT

None of the pieces added up! A strong stench of coffee poisoned the air, blocking and cramming its way into the noses of the people in the room. Not even a pin drop could be heard as they all continued to attempt to solve the case, none of them willing to step forward in their own fears. The case of Anya Livingstone had been underestimated. What you think would've been a normal case had soon spiralled into several sleepless weeks on end, yet here they were again, looking over what they'd already pieced together. Something is just not adding up...

May Cademy-Clementson (11)
Marden High School, North Shields

LOST

Drip, drip, drip. I knew what I did was wrong, but... but why did I do it? Was I drugged? Was I dared? There left no evidence in my brain of why I did this. I couldn't even recall what happened today. I can't even recognise who lies here, dead by my own sinful hands. They're coming for me, I know it. But what will I tell them? No; I have nothing to tell. I have too many commitments. I should run! Now!

"Stop! Raise your hands and get into the car, or otherwise..." a distant voice spoke, and... *boom!*

Ankitha Ramesh (12)
Marden High School, North Shields

YoungWriters Est. 1991

THE MISSING FRIEND

I was at work, at midnight. I had to do a nightshift because my friend who normally works the nightshifts didn't show up. Nobody knows why, so I decided to ask people she knew. They said they didn't know where she was. They said she hadn't talked to them either. It was highly unusual they said, but I had three suspects on hand. They all said the same things; *exactly* the same things. I think they're siblings. I broke into their house, only to find two of them tied up, along with my friend. It was one of the police...

Moumi Fabima (11)
Marden High School, North Shields

UNSOLVED

I was driving down a dark road at night, shadows hanging over the road, my headlights slicing into them. I was called to investigate a crime scene out in the woods, a murder. A body and traces of a scuffle had been found alongside an abandoned car, the doors open, lights still on. The victim was a middle-aged caucasian male with dark hair, wearing a yellow jacket, blue denim jeans and white sneakers. I rounded a corner and stepped out of my car. No; it couldn't be. I recognised that man; he was my older brother. Who would do this?

Heather Marchbank (12)

Marden High School, North Shields

SHOCKED

I spotted something in the forest as I walked through. I stood still and looked down towards the ground as I approached it, trying to work out what it was. I walked up to the object, shocked by what I saw. It was a body. A human body. There was a stab wound right there, where the heart was, and with the knife still in it. I immediately called the police to come and investigate the incident. I froze and waited until they arrived, staring in confusion. Once they were there, they investigated the fingerprints to find the guilty culprit.

Darcy Ridgway (11)
Marden High School, North Shields

THE HARD CALL

It was the hardest decision of my life. I sat there at my pristine desk where the evidence was spread.

I couldn't believe it; I had trusted him. He took advantage and hundreds died. He had done that and I was tasked with bringing him in. Soon, word came through and I dispersed to the office building that loomed over the city.

Once inside, I got to work, weaving my way through the maze of an office to the penthouse where he had been spotted.

I got there.

He had a gun and hostages.

I made the hard call...

Jack Harker (13)
Marden High School, North Shields

THE UNSOLVED CRIME

It was like any other ordinary day, two police officers driving to the coffee shop whilst they were on their break. One of them spotted something on the way back, so they turned around and went to where he saw it. A motionless arm. It was hanging out from behind a wall. They cautiously walked over to where the arm was... It wasn't just an arm, it was a whole body. Not just somebody. It was the body of Helen Wakesmith, whose investigation was so hard, it was just forgotten about. Could this be the start to a new investigation?

Jack Horsham (11)
Marden High School, North Shields

THE TREE OF BLOOD

There lay a tree in the field. One that the suspect grew. I dug up the dirt. Something was wrong. That familiar rancid smell filled the air. This was it. I kept on digging. Then I saw it. The corpses were deformed. The roots grew through them. I could count a total of five. The roots were soaked in dried blood, giving them a flaky brown texture. We had our culprit and evidence. But the culprit had disappeared. No one would have thought he would have done this. And that's how he had gotten away with it three years ago.

Tarah Mawson (13)
Marden High School, North Shields

MISTAKEN SUSPECT

I was woken up to the putrid smell of smoke and the sound of a siren that rang through my head. Fire engulfed the doorway and my only option for survival became to escape through the window. I exited the window where I ended up standing next to a pool of flaming gasoline where I was spotted by an officer. In fear of being arrested, I darted off as quick as my legs could carry me, and ran around the corner and took a left into a nearby alleyway. I ducked behind some bins when somebody came into the alleyway...

Finn O'Brien (12)
Marden High School, North Shields

MYA

I didn't know what to do. One night, I was walking and I saw a symbol on the floor. It looked like a person. There was an arrow, I followed it into some strange woods. I looked and I saw it, where Mya was murdered. That drawing was Mya. I followed more arrows until they stopped. I saw her in my mind when she got killed. There was an arrow pointing to a bit of mud.

I dug. I found a bracelet. I don't know what happened next. I woke to police fanning me to wake me up. Case closed.

Harmony Stavers (11)
Marden High School, North Shields

ANGER

I didn't mean to kill her. It was all in the heat of the moment. It wasn't my fault, was it? The noise of the sirens rang in my ears. I stared down at the body. The shard of glass was plunged deep in her chest, she quivered before the light in her eyes died out. I had killed her; her, my only friend, the only one who had stayed with me when I lashed out. But this time my anger had taken me too far. I sank to my knees and whispered one solitary word: "Goodbye."

Marnie Boden (11)
Marden High School, North Shields

IVY CORPSE

The air was damp. I brushed past the ally and slunk into an old house. The house was smashed and vandalised. I moved to the back and went to find the body. When I got to the back, it was filled with used cigarettes and ivy. The body was in the corner, ivy wrapped around the corpse as though it was a cocoon. His eyes were popping out of his head. It was a fresh kill. I wandered over to the corpse and checked for any other bodies. There was only the one body, but blood everywhere...

Neve Campbell (12)
Marden High School, North Shields

THE MURDER

The blood dripped from the head as the knife was speared through the middle of the head, the face unrecognisable because of the wounds that she had. Hundreds of footprints of blood were around the victim as there were many people at the murder, footprints leading all in different directions but trailing into nothingness.

Her upper intestines were able to be seen from the harsh thrashes and stabs in her body. This murder was planned. What had this innocent girl done?

Daniel Ward (11)
Marden High School, North Shields

WHERE'S CASSIE?

"It's been a couple of days since Cassie went missing, and we only have security cameras and a blood trail," explained Jess. They all followed the trail to find a bloody knife. They all gasped in shock as the realisation hit them, the possibility that she wasn't breathing. They all slowly followed till they found her... lying there motionless, and a piece of paper lay there, opened, saying: 'Never underestimate my power. From ???'

Emma Mills (11)

Marden High School, North Shields

UNSOLVED

One day, Detective Whiterose received a case to investigate a murder at House 4, Maple Road, Indiana. When Detective Whiterose arrived at the house, massive quantities of crimson blood was spilt on the floor. It was a horrific sight. The usually beautiful ornate house looked run-down and abandoned. A young couple in their early twenties lay dead, blood still spilling from their bodies. The woman was pregnant until her untimely demise, her hand still encased in her husband's. Detective Whiterose eventually left. Despite their best efforts, the case was never cracked and their children attended their late parents' funeral.

Evangeline Perry (11)
Perryfields High School, Oldbury

SUSPECT

It just didn't add up. All the pieces fit except this one. The CCTV was correct, the alibi was a bunch of nonsense and still she bleated it wasn't her, over and over. My department had caught her virtually red-handed, but nobody had been found. A family grudge was one thing, but murder was another. As I sat at my desk, pondering over this last piece of the puzzle, my phone buzzed. "Boss?" My second-in-command's panicked voice echoed off the walls.
"Yes?" I answered.
"The suspect, sir, the one we convicted two days ago, well, she's been murdered...!"

Lottie Brooks (13)
Perryfields High School, Oldbury

THE MYSTERY OF THE MENTAL ASYLUM

The mental asylum, an imposing and majestic building that everyone knows, but what happens on the inside? They can only wonder...

The crack in the downstairs window let in the cold night air, along with the noise of the sirens. The flashing blue lights revealed the bodies, drowning in blood, scattering the floor. Crimson splatters all over the white-tiled walls an indication of the chaotic terror that must have taken place.

The crumbling old walls hold so much, witness to the lives of all its residents and staff, and now, more disturbingly, how they met their gruesome ends... here...

Tilly Wise (13)
Perryfields High School, Oldbury

THE HACKER ON THE LOOSE

'10110011' is what the computers showed all over the police stations and prisons in the city. This had been the hack of the century. All the jail cells around the city were wide open as the most dangerous and harmless prisoners fought for their freedom.

It was chaos all over the city. Police backup units were arriving at the crime scenes. The major roads and highways were congested due to emergency response vehicles. I couldn't do anything. It was mayhem and confusion all over the city.

This had been the most successful cyber attack in years, and hopefully the last...

Vusimuzi Ncachiwe (13)
Perryfields High School, Oldbury

THE GHOST DETECTIVE

It was morning...

The detective stood in the dank, musty-smelling alley, staring down at the corpse. Blood was splattered up the moss-covered wall, dripping into a crimson puddle. The detective knelt beside the corpse, searching its pockets for identification. A shiny silver object in the body's pocket caught his eye. He reached in and took it out... It was a police badge similar to his own.

Fearfully, he looked back towards the corpse, realising that he had not seen its face. He turned the body towards him and saw, with horror, his own pale face staring back at him...

Ethan Brooks (12)

Perryfields High School, Oldbury

KILLER IN THE MIRROR

It was a murky, overcast morning - I dreaded another day chasing this animal. Three murders, no evidence, no suspects. Yesterday, forensics had flown around the mournful scene; crimson art was painted all around the dry dusty walls, family pictures hung on the wall. They were cracked and wept heartbroken melodies of its family who ceased to exist anymore.

I wrestled out of bed, knowing I may have to face this again. As I got up and noticed my room... I knew who the killer was. Tears slowly rolled to the ground. My wall, drenched in blood, spelt out: 'It's me'.

Cara Jones (14)
Perryfields High School, Oldbury

MYSTERIOUS ABDUCTIONS

In my school, there are three missing children. After my lesson, I decided to find some information about the kidnapper. I found some footprints leading to a peculiar shed. I felt agitated. The next morning, I rushed to my teacher, in palpitation and anxiousness. I begged my teacher to investigate the shed after school, but there was a man taking the shed. I told the teacher to quickly follow the car and he replied, "Sure." He helped me put on the seatbelt, but something wasn't feeling right. Why was the seatbelt so hard? I saw the teacher smirking beside me...

Taher Etel (12)
Perryfields High School, Oldbury

THE MISSING SHOES

"Guilty!"

It all started earlier that day. I was walking down the street and I heard a police officer shout, "Stop right there, you're under arrest!"

I thought nothing of it at first until a pair of shoes came flying down and hit me straight on my head. I looked up in time to see a hooded man run away.

It all happened so fast. I didn't know what was happening... The next thing I knew, I was in handcuffs and a policeman was shouting, "Anything you say will be held against you in court!"

That's how I'm here...

Evie Thomas (12)

Perryfields High School, Oldbury

THE KILLER WITH NO TRACE

It all started at number 42 where the police and the FBI found the family all dead. There was Mary - mother, George - father, Oliver aged nine, Olive aged four, and the maid. The police were so confused because the killer left no trace, no fingerprints or forced entry.

They investigated every day to find traces, but nothing added up. Two months later, the police found another six families dead about three miles from the Croftens, with the same clues. Then Mr Benson found out that all the families were found dead in the living room, three miles from each other...

Tegan Jeanes (13)
Perryfields High School, Oldbury

THE GIRL IN THE BATHROOM

There's a legend about bathroom 4B. People say that blood drips from the stalls and a demonic ghost lurks in the corners. It's just me though; it's all a prank. That's what I thought till this Christmas. I walked into the bathroom, ready to prank, but I wasn't alone. In the corner, where I normally lurk, there was a figure. Her enchanting ocean-blue eyes and mouth dripped with blood, she was ghostly white, and her silky ebony hair had been pulled out in chunks. I looked into her glistening eyes and my whole body froze, then, black...

Grace Bell (12)
Perryfields High School, Oldbury

THE FIGURE

It just didn't add up. Five men slaughtered. Axe wounds all over, stabbed through the chest and thighs. No weapons, no clues, no lead on whoever did this brutal attack. All of a sudden, I realised the camera was outside, so I decided to check the security footage. When I entered the dark room, I played the footage and saw a blood-soaked figure standing over the river of bodies, with an axe sharper than a tiger's tooth. Suddenly, a message appeared and said: 'All who have done wrong will die.'
Slash! An axe pierced the officer...

Lucas Willacy (12)
Perryfields High School, Oldbury

A NEW NORMAL

Will the world change? Will there be a new beginning? Is this how it was meant to be? Nobody knows. Perhaps the world sees this as a new normal. But the true question remains, what is it? It's the plague amongst us at this very moment, COVID-19, but is there an answer? Maybe our worst nightmare will come true... Maybe our worst nightmare will never leave us alone... Even if it decides to leave, a scar will remain: constantly obsessing over masks, compulsive hand washing, never feeling safe. Do we need to hide our faces from the world any longer?

Afnaan Asnain (12)
Perryfields High School, Oldbury

DARKNESS

He was so mad about what had just happened, he couldn't keep his anger in. He started to kick everything around him, his bed and wardrobe, breaking his wardrobe. His mom, who was downstairs, heard the loud bang from the wardrobe. She slowly walked up the stairs. Something tapped him on the shoulder.

He looked behind him and there was a 7ft *thing* dressed in a black cloak, wearing a plague mask. The man hugged him and then all he could see was darkness. He couldn't see the man or the room. He ran and shouted, looking, but no hope...

Kyle Marklew-Hill (12)
Perryfields High School, Oldbury

UNSOLVED

With the setting sun came a sky of fire, the orange of every wintry hearth. A crisp wind flew, curling and twisting around the bladed palm leaves. It was there the thin, bony body lay, exposed to the alloy-silver reflection of the ascending moon. Irritated with sand, soft, silky water cascaded over the senseless, deceased body, washing away every clue there was to be unravelled. I had no choice other than to give the body to the open, vast mouth of all living things. I watched as it drifted, meaningfully, into the sea. Would the body ever be found again?

Esme Day (13)

Perryfields High School, Oldbury

MURDER MYSTERY

He was going through torture. He had just murdered his best friend. He could never move on from this terrifying night. He had to find a way to leave and never come back. He couldn't ask his mother for money, he was all alone with no money, no home, no life. He'd done things that you wouldn't believe a sixteen-year-old could even do. He'd left home where he had the safety of his mother. It was a night that no other soul could ever forget. He had two breathtaking choices: keep running or surrender and take the punishment he deserves?

Rio Moyo (11)
Perryfields High School, Oldbury

AN OPERATION TOO SIMPLE

The waiter went unnoticed, spiking a glass with clear liquid. This was in fact tetrodotoxin, a deadly poison with no antidote. If done correctly, Hercule Poirot would return home and the poison would only affect him by the time he was asleep. As for himself, once finished, he would be on a flight to New Zealand as a whole different person, with a large sum of money added to his Swiss bank account. The real waiter would wake up with a sachet of tetrodotoxin in his pocket, directly linkable to the murder.
He smiled to himself. It was too easy.

Peter Starkie
Perryfields High School, Oldbury

THE FIFTEEN MURDERS

There has been another murder at the hotel. Fifteen in two weeks. I hope it's the last one. All the victims were from out of town. I had to spend hours looking over the cases, desperate to find a link. I was tired but determined to solve the crimes. After several calls and tracing friends and family, I got it. All the victims had at one time worked as security at Super-Labs, the pharmaceutical giant. They all left the company overnight after having an argument with Barry Long, the boss. I confronted him and got the confession I was after...

Hayden Weston (11)
Perryfields High School, Oldbury

THE PERFECT ESCAPE...

Nobody was meant to know, but he found out. I did what anybody would do to save their reputation. The plan was foolproof. It proceeded like clockwork.

I knew we were doing an experiment on gunpowder, so he left the lab one night and I tampered with the scales. When the next day came and the demo commenced, he added too much and the room filled with a plume of smoke! Thus giving me the perfect time to switch his water bottle with my pre-made cyanide-laced water bottle.

I had to leave for my other lesson which he wasn't in...

Emela Branston (12)

Perryfields High School, Oldbury

MISSING CHILD!

Robert Dunbar was a young boy who went missing at the age of four. This happened in 1912 (the same year as the Titanic sinking). The family went to New York for a little trip (travelling on the Titanic). When the boat sank, everyone but Robert made it safely. The police thought that Robert was dead, but Robert's parents were convinced he was still alive. Or were his parents going crazy? The mother stated that she had spoken to Robert, but people thought she was mentally unstable. Was he alive or dead?
We'll never know...

Lauren Cross (11)
Perryfields High School, Oldbury

THE LOCKDOWN SERIAL KILLER

Wednesday, August the 12th, 1998

'It's been a rough few days. I had to escape from 'them'. They know where I am and I'm sure it's going to be a matter of days until I leave the family. It's priority to keep them safe.'

I found this book in a wardrobe in my aunt's house. I don't think that there has been a day in my life since I found it that I haven't looked at it. I know it's only a few sentences in a book, and yes, I may just be paranoid, but what if I'm not...?

David Akinbode (11)

Perryfields High School, Oldbury

I WAS GOOD

I promise you I was good this time. I cleaned up the blood, disposed of the body appropriately, left no trace. My alibi has to be what I'm proudest of. I have a flawless alibi. No one will ever know, so why am I so paranoid?

She had dug too deep; she knew too much. She had to be silenced. I did what I must. Now my love will stay safe and invisible as she wishes.

I walked into college as normal, I wasn't even a suspect. Her best friend, however, was.

"Guilty!" boomed the judge. Case closed. I win.

Chloe Whitehead (13)
Perryfields High School, Oldbury

LAMP LIGHT

It just didn't add up. There was a robbery at Mr Shamsi's house, but nobody saw the thief, and nothing had been stolen except a lamp. What could be so valuable about a worthless old lamp? Now, normally lamps are just brought to give out light. Then how come only this particular lamp was stolen? It was a mystery!

The next morning, I decided that it was my duty to see if there was any possible clue to help find the guilty person. That was, of course, if the police didn't search the house first! So, wish me luck!

Jensen Warren (11)

Perryfields High School, Oldbury

ME AND MY DEAD WIFE

People think the dead can't talk. I was one of those people until now. Ever since my wife died, I've been hearing voices and I've been seeing her behind me in the mirror. There have been many times I've almost died. It's unexplainable. One time, my house was set on fire. They said it was due to a candle in my living room, but I don't own any candles. That day, I heard someone say, "It was me." I believe it was my wife. She's probably still mad at me, but I had no other choice but to kill her...

Leveah Anning
Perryfields High School, Oldbury

ONE SHOT

A death. A death that could change a town with just one gunshot. The question is, who pulled the trigger? The answer is: anyone. Whether it's the creepy guy who lives next door or the rich blonde girl with blue eyes who all the boys like; anything or anyone is a suspect of a death like what has happened in my town. As for the pretty blonde girl in this story, she's the depressed girlfriend of an innocent boy who was shot between the eyes and left dead in an underground tunnel, but who was guilty of the heart-breaking death?

Sadie Jean (12)
Perryfields High School, Oldbury

THE HACKER

Some people change after being sent to prison. In a prison you've probably never heard of, a devious hacker lived. He has been in prison more times than everyone ever in the prison and left minimal clues in prison escapes.

A prison guard who works at the prison claims 'he never saw how he broke out but saw him run off down the hall with some remote-control dinos'. The only clues at the scene were a laptop and a torch with no batteries.

Whatever the future of this man's plans is, it won't be good...

Alfie Redfern-Webb (12)

Perryfields High School, Oldbury

THE GIRL WHO WAS NEVER FOUND

It just didn't add up. No one could find her, she had disappeared. It has been three days since the disappearance. She was last seen walking home at night. There were search parties all over the town, but no one ever found anything, not even a bit of evidence. They looked at cameras and asked local people, but no one had a clue where she could've wandered off to. She mentioned to me that she was scared of a white van that had followed her home after school. Although no one could ever find any evidence of this white van...

Georgia Byfield-Cable (13)
Perryfields High School, Oldbury

UNSOLVED MURDER

Detectives and police got a call to investigate a crime scene immediately at 103 Trips Lane. The arrival was unpleasant. Blood was dripping down the walls while two dead bodies were lying on the floor. How did this happen? This was probably not the holiday the Miller family had in mind, with a murderer still on the loose. It was getting late.

Three hours had passed and no clues were discovered, so the investigation carried on the following morning. Still no clues. If any clues are found, investigations will start again.

Lauren Moores (12)
Perryfields High School, Oldbury

REVENGE

They had picked on me my whole life. It was finally time I gave in to the fact that I couldn't take it anymore, but I never expected it to go this way. Blood everywhere, my head filled with questions: *do I call the police? Do I run and leave them to bleed to death?* Overwhelmed with thoughts, I raced to the nearest puddle and washed away the evidence when I heard a distressed voice. I'd been caught. They had seen too much. I closed my eyes, leaving the lifeless body of my second victim dead on the floor!

Grace Brown (13)
Perryfields High School, Oldbury

THE UNDERCOVER GIRL

It was Friday and I was at my friend's party. There were drinks. I took one too many. Eventually drunk, I started feeling loopy, swinging a knife up in the air. *Kaboom!* I had stabbed Jake by accident! Lucy called the police. I heard sirens down the road. I ran to the bathroom, washed the blood off my hands and changed my outfit to fit in with the crowd. The police did not suspect me at all. Then everyone knew me as the 'undercover girl'! That is the story of my life, but something had to happen...

Simran Kaur Sandhu (11)

Perryfields High School, Oldbury

THE UNSOLVED ROBBERY

A robbery had occurred in a cold winter. Thousands were stolen. Workers and police officers checked security cameras, it had been seen that the thief fled in a black car. The thief's description was a black beard, a red coat, and he was at least 5" 11. The police had found six suspects. Three of the six were set free, but the remaining three were still under suspicion. One more had been set free because he was wearing a red jacket, not a coat. The remaining two were kept captive as the mystery was unsolved.

Ellie Shier (12)
Perryfields High School, Oldbury

WASHED-UP MURDER

I'm a police officer who was called to a murder scene at a beach in England. I am required to document everything that happened at that beach.

So, it was 7:26am on a Saturday morning. I had just left my house when I got a call to go to the beach near my house. That was my first time seeing the rotting washed-up corpse on the dirty sand. The body had many stab wounds and purple bloated skin.

There was no clue as to the murderer apart from footprints leading to a shack. There was a man inside...

Ethan Elliott (11)
Perryfields High School, Oldbury

THE INKY MYSTERY

As always, there was a crime scene... but this was not a normal one... This had ink and blood. Oh, I forgot to introduce myself... I am Detective Cheese, but you can call me Mr Cheese. This ink was fresh and I found a trail and it almost looked like footprints, so... I followed them.
I followed them for hours, but nothing was getting closer. That was when I heard squelching... It was getting closer and louder. Then that's when there was a gigantic inky monster with claws like knives, so I ran...

Josh Messer (12)
Perryfields High School, Oldbury

THE MURDERER ZACH!

There was a man called Zach. He was a very happy man with a wife and two children, and he had one best friend and his name was Adam. One day, his best friend backstabbed him and called one of his gangster friends to kidnap him and his children. When they kidnapped Zach, he was wondering what happened, and when he found out that Adam set him up, he was figuring out how to get out of the warehouse.

A couple of days later, he found a way out. Then he got back home, leaving the house to kill Adam...

Kai'sean Mattis (12)
Perryfields High School, Oldbury

EVIDENCE

It just did not add up... For months, I had been trying to solve a robbery crime made in a bank, but all the clues did not make sense! Some showed a photograph of someone running out of the same robbed bank, and another showed the same person shopping at the same time. This was the weirdest crime I had ever had! I was about to give up until I heard a booming crash coming from the antique shop next door. I came out to have a look and it was the same person robbing the shop from my evidence!

Megan Sanders (11)
Perryfields High School, Oldbury

WRONG PLACE, WRONG TIME

I knew it was wrong. I didn't want to do it, but I had to. Dean said that all I had to do was steal one item and I would be in. As I breathed out calmingly, I jumped and grabbed hold of the fence and hauled myself over. As I approached the house, I broke out into a cold sweat. Quietly, I slid open the window and climbed inside. I searched around for anything valuable, which was when I saw it. The woman had been stabbed. I pulled out the knife, then I heard the sirens. I was stuck...

Evie Morris (13)
Perryfields High School, Oldbury

FOREVER

Tears, pain, regret. All the things I felt when I did it. I did not mean to, I... just did. I was not right. I couldn't understand what happened, it just went by like a flash.

Tears, pain, anger. All the things they felt, the family. They hated me. *I* hated me. I had just had the best night and was ready to sleep when she came in, shouting. I was scared, terrified. I reacted... *Bam!* Her head hit the floor and she was gone forever. My love gone. Forever.

Oliver Kapasi (13)
Perryfields High School, Oldbury

A DREAM?

I woke up with a sudden urge. My hands were cuffed to the bars on what looked like a prison bed. Did they find me? Did they find the weapons? Am I in jail? My heart dropped as a police officer walked past the room I was in. Struggling for help, I realised my mouth was taped up. That was the last thing I ever remembered from that day...

Again, I suddenly woke up, but in my own room this time. Was it a dream? Am I in trouble? I'll never know.

Unsolved.

Dexter Gooding (11)

Perryfields High School, Oldbury

UNSOLVED

I was waiting around the corner for my prey. My boss said he had escaped many of the best bounties, and I was the best one. So, back to the scene. I was there, waiting for my bounty to come out of the hotel since one of the detectives gave me the time he was going to leave. I moved in on my target and, to my surprise, he was already one step ahead of me as he sent out a smoke bomb to distract me. Then, when the smoke cleared, he was gone, he just vanished...

Alexander Jongwe (12)

Perryfields High School, Oldbury

NIGHTMARE MURDERER

4:15am. Slick shadows surrounded my rock-solid bed. "Guilty," the judge's voice screamed in my ears. "Guilty." It's happening again.

"Guilty."

I don't want to go back...

Hundreds sat in front of me in the bland courtroom. Rough hands pressed on my shoulders as I rested in a chair.

A resonant voice raised in the large room: "Caroline Smith was killed at 4:15am in her own home." A broad, pale man stood tall in the judge's bench. "A nine-inch dagger was plunged in her chest with the fingerprints of Mark Smith." Sweat trickled down my head. "I declare him guilty!" 4:16am.

Courtney Rigby (14)

Rugby Free Secondary School, Rugby

THE DEADLY WILL

"My sister's dead body was found in my dressing room!"
"We know. We ask you to calm down, ma'am. Is there anything that you've witnessed?"
"You think I killed my sister?"
"Ma'am, Abriana Alamanni's death is being investigated and everyone's being interviewed. From what we have gathered, your father wanted to change his will and leave everything to Abriana. The murder also happened just before he signed it?"
"Yes. Giovanni, my father's best friend, told me about the will and how he found out he was originally supposed to be a part of it too."
"Giovanni knew about the change...?"

Wiktoria Groszewska (13)
Rugby Free Secondary School, Rugby

SAVE IT FOR THE JUDGE

"I'm innocent, please!" I screamed as they pushed me against the hard brick wall.

Sweat was dripping down my head, my heart racing. Why did they think I was the thief? I would never steal! Oh well, nothing I could say would change their mind.

"Hey, stop dreaming."

"I'm not dreami-"

"Shush it, now!"

I still couldn't believe it. Why was I being arrested? I did nothing. Nothing!

Why wouldn't they believe me? I'm not a thief. Why would I steal? I thought. Wait... I was saying this aloud.

"Excuse me, miss. I-"

"Sorry!"

"Save it for the judge."

Madison Bramwell (11)
Rugby Free Secondary School, Rugby

LOST BUT NOT YET FOUND

...It was time.

Two months later...

It was almost a week from when reports had reached the police station for a 15-year-old missing teen named Linda Wilson, last seen at Dawson Community Academy. Officer James had contacted the border agency as requested by her mother for any information.

Next day...

Ring! Mrs Wilson's phone rang in the morning. Not knowing who it was, she answered. It turned out to be the local police with news.

"Morning, ma'am, we have found your daughter in Rochester Woods..."

Little did they know, it wasn't their daughter... but the killer.

Nadia Barnor (12)

Rugby Free Secondary School, Rugby

DEATH'S BEACH

Three kids were playing on a beach. One went on a wander, wishing they hadn't.
She noticed a trail of red coming from the fishing shed. Looking closer, she noticed the darkness of the shade of red. It definitely looked like blood, or could it be paint? Shouting to her friends, they opened the door, a body on the floor, fishing rod impaled in the chest. They stopped in their tracks, mortified, ringing the police.
The detective came, gathering clues, removing the body:
'Female
25
Scars
Fishing pole in the chest
No ID.'
Another body, different place? thought Detective Banner...

Hannah Parrish (12)
Rugby Free Secondary School, Rugby

THE MAID FALLS

When Joan's burned alive, we will watch them carefully - not the lady in the flame, but Goodman Philip.

Our knights captured her outside Conpinue and took her to Philip. As the Duke of Burgundian, he was finally face-to-face with the LaPucelle, the strongest propaganda weapon of his enemy.

"You're nothing but the traitor of France!" Joan roared. "But I'm a patriot." Philip gave no reply. When the English delivered the 10,000 coins, he handed her to them.

There she is now, the fire's lit. This execution will be like everything in this world: just a way to achieve a goal...

Jason Zhang (15)
Rugby Free Secondary School, Rugby

THE MYSTERY OF THE HORRID TEACHER

Harry stood up. "You see, she was eating her snack, probably little children, and heard clattering: knives being sharpened and whispers. She thought they were ghosts and was yelling at the sounds. She never realised that her death bed was calling.

The murderers struck quickly. Forensics found a strand of potato peel in a wound. The knives came from the kitchen and only three people were in there that day. Miss Alshawe, Mrs Ruddor and Mr Wolker."

Harry cleared his throat. "Mrs Ruddor and Mr Wolker, together you killed Miss Gretchin."

"She had it coming!" they cried and ran away.

Ashton Castleton (12)

Rugby Free Secondary School, Rugby

MY SWEETEST COUSIN

My cousin's case has been open for eleven years.

Each March seemed to go so slowly, as I was persistently haunted by melancholic moments of springtimes - Colette smiling while doing dishes she passionately despised or letting out tiny giggles from the slightest amusement she'd encounter.

I withdrew from my troubled conscience... But the air would stay perturbed, in this house, in this room, whether or not I was pondering how *they* didn't know.

My mind focused on the buzzing of the desk's light. I scoffed, starting to smile at my hands.

How did they never taste her in the cake?

Patricija Biseniece (13)

Rugby Free Secondary School, Rugby

DETECTIVE'S DOOM

"Lock down the south entrance!" I order, after discovering another clue from the bank heist three days ago. Working non-stop since the heist has paid off. Catching the criminals will be simple; all we have to do is stop them fleeing south, and intercept them before they find another escape and slip away silently like they normally do.

"We have the barricade set now, sir," I have been informed. Now we have the criminals cornered...

A loud noise in the background wakes the detective.

"You are the detective who spoils my every plot. Not anymore." The criminal pulls the trigger.

Jonathan Middleton (15)
Rugby Free Secondary School, Rugby

A BETRAYAL

Money was scattered over the floor, alarms blaring. The criminals were still there, hiding in the cracks.
"Where are you?" Detective James bellowed in a gruff voice. Sergeant Cassell crept round each corner, wary of what might jump out. A muddy footprint lay beneath the mess. Detective James inspected and photographed the evidence. A shadow of boots swept across his eyes.
"Sir, they are on the run!" Sergeant called. The detective ran for the one in sight, but little did he know who was behind him. Cassell was behind, gun in hand. A shot was fired, piercing the detective's heart...

Cailey Adams (14)

Rugby Free Secondary School, Rugby

MAFIA AND MURDER!

The door, tall and painted white with a small peephole, burst under the intense weight of the mafia gang standing outside. The leader, Allie Doyle, walked in with a pistol in hand, walking through rooms, and found a woman in the bathroom, curled in a ball. Allie called out, "What are you doing in here?"

All she could say was, "Don't kill me... please!" Allie looked disgusted.

"I hate when people beg..." Allie said. The other people in the gang were waiting outside the house. Allie's twin sister, Franky, was among them. The last thing they heard was: *bang...*

Leah Chamberlain (13)

Rugby Free Secondary School, Rugby

THE BUTCHER

I heard manic laughter and screams. A thick mass of coagulated liquid began to appear. I noticed it was flesh, human flesh and blood. *What is this?* I wondered.

I reached the source of the screams; a boy was tied to a metal slab. A dark figure towered over him hacking his leg with a machete! I tackled the figure, knocking the knife from his grasp.

"Why?" I screamed...

"Cannibalism," he shrieked. He calmly explained he was kidnapping children, butchering and selling them. As he laughed manically, I couldn't restrain him any longer. I felt a knock to my head...

Charlee O'Meara (15)
Rugby Free Secondary School, Rugby

A SHADOW IN THE WOODS

Hunting owls hooted from moonlit treetops as the ground shuddered from cold winds. The intrigued detectives investigated as blood trickled across the floor. As the detectives were investigating, trying to find the cause of the young man's death, a shadow lurked around them. They did not realise this until it was too late. The shadow leapt out! The throat of a detective slit. His colleague collapsed on the floor; both dead, abandoned in the dark, cold forest. As the shadow vanished, it whispered, "All who enter my forest will die an unholy death and your souls with be mine forever."

Lucy Carlyon (12)
Rugby Free Secondary School, Rugby

SWING SET

Walking, the air made my face tingle in the cold. I was surrounded by nature. Birds were singing. The boats just over the hedge are floating down the canal - the sound of water splashing in their wake. Months before, the leaves, now crumbling beneath my feet, filled the trees with wonderous colour. For that moment, I was at peace. Then everything changed...

"Did you do it?"

One question resounded in my head. They described the murder I had essentially committed. Did I *really* do this? He was so young. A small child on a swing set. *Just moments to live...*

Lilly Barker (13)

Rugby Free Secondary School, Rugby

THE DETECTIVE

"Detective Morrison, I've found something!" I yelled from across the room of the crime scene. It was dark and gloomy. A single light bulb hung from the ceiling, swinging back and forth over Mr Johnson's cold, motionless body as he lay in a puddle of blood. It was vile. I shouldn't even be here right now, but unfortunately, I'm the main suspect. I had to do whatever it took to prove my innocence.

"It's a journal." I held it, feeling nauseous, I flipped it open to see a note he wrote with the last of his energy: 'It was Morrison'...

Niamh Evans (13)
Rugby Free Secondary School, Rugby

12:07

12:07. A night I would always remember.

Me and my friend Jonathan went to a party to celebrate our boy's eighteenth birthday but little did we know this night was no joke.

We went in and straight up felt a sense of foreboding in our veins. We took four steps, four fearless steps.

Red liquid spilt over the floor like we were travelling through Hell... We tried to leave... A gunshot was fired. *Pow!*

Jonathan was shot... I'd be next. Everyone at the party was killed, like the Purge had been released that night... I was next. Hell was raised...

Emanuele Paval (13)

Rugby Free Secondary School, Rugby

HINDSIGHT IS A WONDERFUL THING

You see a lot when you're sat on a park bench. Kids kicking and screaming as they're reluctantly dragged away by fathers with cautious eyes that scan the park, bearing a look of fear as they appear unfit to parent. It's nothing unusual, not even when the kid resorts to bawling about how this man isn't her father. It's not strange when he shakes his head and smiles at people as if to say 'kids, huh?' before leading them away. It's nothing odd: kids being kids. Until a distraught woman runs up, begging to know if I've seen her daughter...

Eliona Seraj (16)
Rugby Free Secondary School, Rugby

THE MIDNIGHT ROBBERY

The shadow at the door became visible. It was midnight, I was alerted by my intuition that there was something wrong. Sweat formed as my curiosity overcame any sense. The footsteps got closer, it all went black...

Aware that there were cameras, I watched my approach, keeping an eye out. I believed I'd be captured, as sirens slipped by dangerously close. I started running like I was in an Olympic race, the sirens began to fade into the distance. We received an anonymous tip. A figure had been spotted near the crime scene. Action was needed immediately...

Arani Niranjan (12)
Rugby Free Secondary School, Rugby

THE DISASTER LIFE COULD NOT PREDICT

The body in the river. The blood on the rock.

"I have an alibi..."

"...Run!"

Alex Brown, the innocent but dead. Liam Low, the suspect. The class expedition to the woods of the dead.

Everything was normal till they stopped at the river. A shadowy, dark figure scampered through the woods as it took the other two girls one by one. Only Liam and Alex were left.

Alex looked around cautiously for the others. He was pushed into the river and his head hit a rock. He was now dead. But why? Liam was now alone, or so he thought...

Keeley Prestidge (12)

Rugby Free Secondary School, Rugby

THE GREAT LAUNDRY ESCAPE

Day 648

I could no longer continue to stay there. The prison life had broken me. I was a shadow of the man I once was, just surviving by following my soul. There was a glimmer of hope though. It could work; I must believe.

Yesterday, it was gruelling having to break from the kitchen job but laundry was the only way. After a few weeks, I obtained my goal: lying underneath the sheets and the bedding was hot and stuffy.

The road was bumpy, throwing the mailcart around the van. I didn't mean to harm, but now I'm free.

Coby Smith (11)

Rugby Free Secondary School, Rugby

NO SAFETY

The dead can't talk, or so I thought.

Two hours ago, I turned fifteen. I was told my parents had been killed, but I knew it wasn't true. Something my dad once said was: "One day, we'll leave your life. Don't look for us." I knew now was that time.

Two weeks had passed when I got a gun in the mail. And a note, which seemed to be written in my mother's handwriting, read: 'For your safety...'

That night, I saw a figure. I knew then that I would need the gun... I needed it to take someone's life.

Bethan Pybus (14)
Rugby Free Secondary School, Rugby

THE SILENT PATIENT

I'm a female therapist in a town. You wouldn't believe all the cries for help people have in this town. I'm a good person and don't like seeing people get hurt.

One of my patients had accused her husband of an affair.

I woke up at 3am to the phone ringing, knowing no good was going to come. It was Mrs Brown. "They found his body," she cried.

Looking down at the phone, it was covered in blood, as were my hands. "Not again," I muttered to myself. Revenge is best served cold and so was Mr Brown's body...

Shakira Rogrigues-Fahrina (14)
Rugby Free Secondary School, Rugby

COMING

The shadows eat away at what is left of the girl, hiding the savaged remains of the innocent child.

Words are carelessly splattered on the wall: 'I am coming'.

Coming? How could they know where I am? And yet, now, as I stare at the words, I know they will find me like they have many times before.

I can still feel the agonising pain, the only visible scars on my hands bringing back unwanted memories.

I'll die knowing I will finally be punished for the murder of the little girl rotting in the corner, and the many before her.

Amelia Richardson (14)
Rugby Free Secondary School, Rugby

THE UNKNOWN MURDER

I heard screams, cries from the house next door and I knew something wasn't right. I grabbed my coat and hat to explore what was making the noise. As I knocked on the door, no one answered. I knocked louder again but no one answered.

All of a sudden, I heard a click and the door swung open. I stepped into the house. Everything went black.

I'm not sure what happened that day but I've never forgotten it. My story still goes around the village. Some people say they hear more and more screams coming from the house every night.

Imogen Page (13)

Rugby Free Secondary School, Rugby

TRUE JUSTICE

I walk out of the police station. Oh God, they think I did it. No one believes me when I tell them the truth. *Do you mean to say*, they contemplated sceptically, *that you waited* three days *to contact police?* When I explained that I thought the killer was watching, I got the feeling they wanted to laugh in my face.

Now, I close my eyes angrily. Justice; all it is is an excuse. I arrive at the house where it happened, retrieving the gun from the postbox. If you want true justice, you have to take it for yourself...

Steffi Moser (13)
Rugby Free Secondary School, Rugby

HIDING

It starts at the end. A husband found dead, shrouded in mystery. A family torn apart by betrayal. A note, leaving out no secrets, told the story of a cheating husband, who now lay lifeless on the floor surrounded by a growing pool of blood. Nobody can lose that amount of blood and live.
In the next room, the wife who'd just signed off the note was tending to her defensive injuries. She started to leave a trail of false evidence, enough to keep the DIs going in circles long after she'd fashioned herself a new life and lived it.

Thomas Jebson (15)
Rugby Free Secondary School, Rugby

THE CHILD...

I just got out of the bathroom of a nearby restaurant, and a young lady came to me and asked me, "Would you mind keeping an eye on my child while I go to the bathroom?" She had already left, so I couldn't say no. The kid looked at me, he had beautiful green eyes and rosy red lips. He looked tired and scared. He whispered something, the only thing I heard was, "In trouble." I ignored it.

Hours later, I was in the holding cell. I'd been arrested, the young lady accused me of kidnapping. Then the kid spoke...

Anastasia Gkika (12)
Rugby Free Secondary School, Rugby

THE MURDER NEXT DOOR

Hey, I'm Delilah Jones, and my life is strange.

You may be wondering what I mean. Well, it started like any normal day: woke up, got dressed, went to school. Then I got home...

We had a new neighbour. There was something strange about this man. I went over and said, "Hey, I'm Delilah Jones, what's your name?"

That night, he appeared at my window. That was the end of me.

The police are still investigating my death, but I know he's left town. I haunt him every day. He will pay for what he did...

Bethany Bradshaw (13)
Rugby Free Secondary School, Rugby

THE CUPBOARD

"Guilty!"

I didn't mean to do it. I didn't mean to kill her. My mother was in labour. That night, I stayed at home whilst my dad was with my mum in the hospital. Aisley stayed round, but mum told her she had to go as her gran fell down the stairs. I was alone. I heard rustling in the bushes. I peeked my head through the door, it was my cat. A figure appeared behind me.

The cupboard reeked for days. Now, Aisley is being mourned in the graveyard. I'm flooded with guilt. I'll always remember that day...

Holly Prestidge (13)

Rugby Free Secondary School, Rugby

VANISHED!

I knew there was something strange going on in my neighbourhood. People were disappearing. I didn't take much notice but made sure I was careful. I hadn't been out for ages and decided to go for a quick run. That was my biggest mistake. There were hardly any cars about. The road was almost always busy. I headed home after sunset with a strange feeling that I was being followed. I turned around to see a van, the same one that the police were looking for. The door slid open and it became obvious that I was the next victim...

Zainab Malik (13)

Rugby Free Secondary School, Rugby

THE UNSOLVED ATTACK

It was a cold, windy night. Just then, we noticed that only seconds were left until the bank would be completely wiped out. All I could do was pray that they didn't find us and the police would get here quickly. I could hear everything they said. They were saying that they were going to be putting bombs around the building. When the police arrived, they would set them off.

At this point I knew I had to do something, but no, it was too late. Together, we started running to the door. Only I got out - nobody else survived.

Dominik Tarnowski (13)
Rugby Free Secondary School, Rugby

VELVET TIGER

Hello there. My name is Velvet Tiger and I am one of the FBI's most wanted.

You might be wondering why I'm talking to you all. You probably all hate me for the murders I have committed. Well, I don't blame you, not at all.

Today I will commit one last murder and that murder will be mine. I have spent nine days running from the FBI since I killed Justin.

The pressure is on, I can hear the dogs and the guns being reloaded.

Goodbye world, it's my death day.

Gunshot.

Rafi Khan (12)
Rugby Free Secondary School, Rugby

THE TAPE

I looked at my hands. The blood was there but the memory wasn't. The last thing I remember was talking to the boss and then he was on the floor.

I turned and ran. I grabbed the key for the security room and unlocked the door. I was looking for a copy of the tape. The tape was missing. In its place, a note: 'You have been framed. Everyone thinks it was you. You shouldn't have given me so much pain'.

The last sound I heard was a gunshot. Blood began seeping through my shirt. It was the end.

Brooke Herrington (12)
Rugby Free Secondary School, Rugby

JEFF DANPER

As soon as I entered the crime scene, I could see blood all over the walls and ceiling. The stench of death hit me. In the middle of the scene was the mangled-up body of the victim, Kuro Takahashi, a 25-year-old Japanese male.

The murder matched all of the ones before it. There was no mistaking it; this was the work of Jeff Danper. He escaped from a mental hospital one month ago and we've had trouble with these deaths and trying to find him ever since. We just have to try and find him, if we can that is...

Jackie Williams (14)
Rugby Free Secondary School, Rugby

FINAL MOMENTS!

Here I am. Moments away from my life ending. Family watching from the other side. I cannot see them, but I can feel them. The force of them rushing through my veins. I feel a small prick in my arm. Then my breathing slows. My pulse weakens. I am just waiting for the moment that the phone rings. But it will never ring. Staring at a light, my vision is getting blurry. The constant reminder in my head for what I have done. The dread of the memories. But the thing is, I did not commit murder. I am *innocent!*

Jack Pearson (15)
Rugby Free Secondary School, Rugby

YOUR MOVE

I'd found a clue. The only question was, to what? By my foot sat a pristine cube of glass, encased within: a perfectly preserved human heart. I moved my torch closer and saw two words engraved into the surface.

I wasn't one to be easily spooked. In fact, I was the hardest one in my family to scare - trust me, they tried. Yet it felt as if a metal band was tightening around my chest, cutting off my air.

I turned and fled. Those two words burned into the back of my mind - 'Your move'.

Elise Richardson (15)
Rugby Free Secondary School, Rugby

1987

Let me tell you about the night on December 15th, 1987. I was coming into the station ready for my next case when I heard a report of a robbery over the radio. I rushed over to the CCTV in the main station. But when I turned to see the CCTV, all I saw was darkness... Nothing but darkness. It was odd but then suddenly the lights turned on to reveal a ransacked shop with nothing left to show for it...
But something caught my eye in the corner of the shop. It was... It was... It was me!

Annalise Baldock (12)
Rugby Free Secondary School, Rugby

Young Writers®
Est. 1991

YOUNG WRITERS INFORMATION

We hope you have enjoyed reading this book – and that you will continue to in the coming years.

If you're a young writer who enjoys reading and creative writing, or the parent of an enthusiastic poet or story writer, visit our website **www.youngwriters.co.uk/subscribe** to join the World of Young Writers and receive news, competitions, writing challenges, tips, articles and giveaways! There is lots to keep budding writers motivated to write!

If you would like to order further copies of this book, or any of our other titles, then please give us a call or order via your online account.

Young Writers
Remus House
Coltsfoot Drive
Peterborough
PE2 9BF
(01733) 890066
info@youngwriters.co.uk

Join in the conversation!
Tips, news, giveaways and much more!

 YoungWritersUK   @YoungWritersCW   YoungWritersCW